Ripple Grove
Press
Portland, OR
RippleGrovePress.com

First Edition 2018
Library of Congress Control Number 2017953921
ISBN 978-0-9990249-1-1

1 2 3 4 5 6 7 8 9 10
Printed in China

This book was typeset in Adobe Caslon Pro.
The illustrations were rendered in pencil and watercolor.
Book design by Melissa Larson

Thank you for reading.

For my girls, Lila, Reese, and Hazel—C. W. R.

For Mom & Dad, who give my ropes a tug on the regular—M. L.

Iver &
Ellsworth

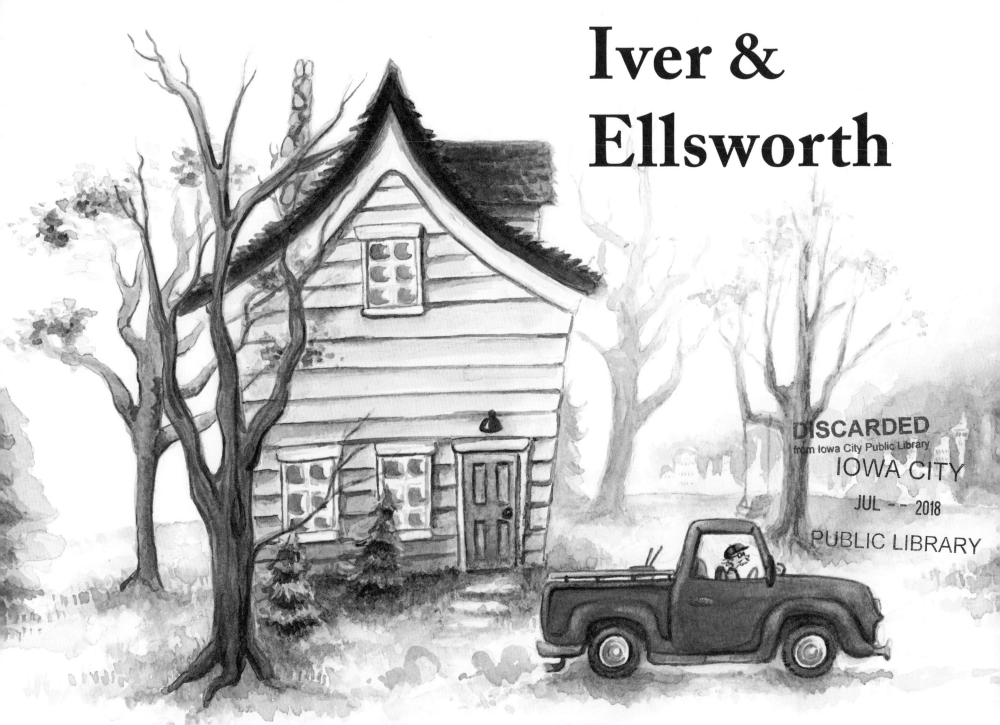

by Casey W. Robinson • illustrated by Melissa Larson

Ripple Grove
Press

ELLSWORTH IS A ROOFTOP BEAR.

Underneath him, a factory hums
and a man bustles.

The man's name is Iver.
Iver and Ellsworth are good friends.

At noon Iver climbs the stairs
to the factory roof.

"Good afternoon, old pal," he says to the giant bear.

Iver carefully unpacks his lunch—
first a cloth napkin, then an apple, and finally,
hummus on whole wheat.

During lunch, Iver and Ellsworth spend a few
minutes taking in the familiar view.

Iver shakes his head at the zipping cars and trucks below.
"Everyone's going somewhere," he says. "We can see the whole world
from up here. That's enough somewhere for me."

Before he returns to work, Iver always makes sure that Ellsworth looks his best.

In the spring, Iver wipes away streaks
of rain on Ellsworth's legs.

In summertime, Iver carefully
shines Ellsworth's paws.

In the fall, Iver plucks the crunchy
leaves that stick to Ellsworth's tummy.

In wintertime, Iver gently shakes the
snow from Ellsworth's shoulders.

Then Iver tugs on the ropes that keep Ellsworth steady.

"Good." He nods. "Good."

Ellsworth's head bobs happily, and his giant paws wave back and forth.

From the highway a car honks hello.

One day, Iver is slow to pack his lunch.

He is slow to drive to work.

He is even slower climbing
the stairs to the factory roof.

Iver sits quietly next to Ellsworth. Then he clears his throat.

"I'm retiring today, old pal," he says. "Seems I'm off to a new somewhere."

Iver tugs on Ellsworth's ropes one last time.

"I'm going to miss you," he says.

"Ellsworth!"

Iver secures the ropes that keep Ellsworth steady, and the two friends take in the new familiar view.

"We can see the whole world from up here. Seems we've found our new somewhere, old pal."

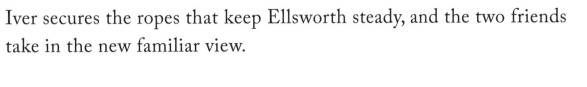

Ellsworth's head bobs happily, and
his giant paws wave back and forth.

From the road a car honks hello.

"Good." Iver nods. "Very good."